T0106423

A Soul Deep Within

Vol. I

Auriette Symone

authorHOUSE®

AuthorHouse™
1663 Liberty Drive
Bloomington, IN 47403
www.authorhouse.com
Phone: 1-800-839-8640

©2009. Auriette Symone. All rights reserved

No part of this book may be reproduced, stored in a retrieval system, or transmitted by any means without the written permission of the author.

First published by AuthorHouse 05/26/2009

ISBN; 1-9781-4389-9018-7

Printed in the United States of America
Bloomington, Indiana

This book is printed on acid-free paper.

I would first like to thank God for giving me the talent and wisdom to write this book. I would like to thank my family for their love and support. I would especially like to thank the women in my family. The first I would like to thank is my mother Prophetess Elizabeth Hollman, both of my aunts Pastor Prophetess Patsy Moultrie and Evangelist Brenda Thomas. The woman I would like thank most of all is my late grandmother Elder Rebecca Davenport. Thank you all for your support. I cannot forget my sisters and my brother, Tequila Porter, Rebecca Porter, and Robert Porter. I also would like to thank my best friend, Syctrilas Smith. I would also like to thank my godmother Evangelist Jacqueline Atkins. Thank you for encouraging me. Thank you for correcting me when I was wrong and praising me when I was right. Most importantly I want to dedicate this book to my son Vycktor A. Prim. He is the bright spot in my life. Finally I would like to dedicate this book to the man I fell in love with. Thank you for teaching me the most important lesson in my life which is being in love is alright, but even love has its place in everyone's life.

God

God almighty

God of love

God in the heavens up above

God of endurance

God of assurance

God of love

God of joy

A God that cares

A God that shares

A God that will always be there

I'm so glad to say

God had mercy upon me today

Oh what joy

When born unto us the baby boy

God will be a friend

Until the end

I will raise up a nation

I'm looking for a people who will obey

People who will take heed and listen to what I say

I will raise up a nation

I'm looking for a people who want to run a race

And get ready to meet the savior face to face

I will raise up a nation

I'm looking for a people who are willing to work

People who's willing to come out filth and dirt

I will raise up a nation

I'm looking for a people with love deep within

People who are willing to come out of sin

I will raise up a nation

I am Rosepetal

I am the one

That's desirable

I am the one

That will set your soul on fire

I am Rosepetal

Yeah that's me

I am the one

That brings the sunshine

I am the one

That is your lover for a lifetime

I am Rosepetal

Yeah that's me

I am the one

That will give you the stars and the moon

I am the one

That dazzles men with her perfume

I am Rosepetal

Yeah that's me

I am the one

That's like fine wine

I am the one

That gets better with time

I am Rosepetal

Yeah that's me

I am the one

That walks with respect

I am the one

That will always watch your back

I am Rosepetal

Yeah that's me

I am the one

That they call Ms. Sexy

I am the one

In my life nothing goes lacking

I am Rosepetal

Yeah that's me

I am the one

That they call Big Baby

I am the one

That carries herself as a lady

I am Rosepetal

Yeah that's me

I am the one

That walks with confidence and pride

I am the one

That takes great stride

I am Rosepetal

Yeah that's me

I am the one

That is educated

I am the one

For anything I am situated

I am Rosepetal

Yeah that's me

I am the one

That will rock your boat

I am the one

That will make your spirit float

I am Rosepetal

Yeah that's me

I am the one

That you love to love

I am the one

That will fight for you when push comes to shove

I am Rosepetal

Yeah that's me

I am the one

That every man wants

I am the one

My body I love to flaunt

I am Rosepetal

Yeah that's me

I am the one

The finest of the fine the best of the best

I am the one

The only one North, South, East, or West

I am Rosepetal

Yeah that's me

I am the one

That will get you high

I am the one

That will make you sigh

I am Rosepetal

Yeah that's me

I am the one

That will make you shout

I am the one

That removes all doubt

I am Rosepetal

Yeah that's me

I am the one

That uses her sex appeal

I am the one

That make men squeal

I am Rosepetal

Yeah that's me

I am the one

Boy you better recognize

I am the one

Boy you know you can't deny

I am Rosepetal

Yeah that's me

I am the one

You're lucky to find

I am the one

Words cannot define

I am Rosepetal

Yeah that's me

I am the one

That is a brick house

I am the one

That represents the dirty dirty south

I am Rosepetal

Yeah that's me

I am the one

That makes your man say ooh

I am the one

That your man wants to be next to

I am Rosepetal

Yeah that's me

I am Rosepetal

You must admit

I am the one

You will never forget

I Want Out

I want out

Out of the constant lying and pain

Out of the constant crying and game

Out of the constant fake relationships

Out of the constant fake friendships

Out of the constant let downs

Out of the constant all too genuine frowns

Are you paying attention

Or by myself do I need to make that decision

I want out

Out of the constant closing in of the walls

Out of the constant stumbles and falls

Out of the constant need for a man

Out of the constant need for a plan

Out of the constant world of depression

Out of the constant thinking of oppression

Are you even concerned

Or are you the things I am saying you are not able to discern

I want out

Out of the constant stereotype

Out of the constant struggle and fight

Out of the constant statistics

Out of the constant chooses and picks

Out of the constant losing of battles

Out of the constant willingness to settle

Does anyone out there care

Or is it your emotions you aren't willing to share

I want out

Out of the constant cold

Out of the constant lies that are told

Out of the constant styles

Out of the constant fake smiles

Out of the constant pretense

Out of the constant lack of sense

Will you listen to me

Or is it just air that I am speaking

I want out

Out of the constant trial and tribulation

Out of the constant demands and stipulation

Out of the constant me using you and you using me

Out of the constant longing to be free

Out of the constant trying to gain your love

Out of life's constant pushes and shoves

I'm trapped in a box

Without a key for it to be unlocked

I want out

Out of the constant trying to live in your shadow

Out of these I call life's constant hardships and battles

Out of life's constant pains and sickness

Somebody, somewhere can I please get a witness

Out of life's constant hustle and bustle

Out of constantly being just a little too subtle

Out of today's constant harsh reality

Out of the cosmic's constant fatality

I want out

That's all I'm going to say

Some of you don't care anyway

My Black Pearl

I know someone

That I call

My black pearl

My black pearl

Was there for me

When I took my first steps

As I grew older

My black pearl

Gave the advice I needed

My black pearl

You are very

Special pearl to me

You may not

Think so

But you are loved

When I'm in trouble

You, no matter what it is

My black pearl sees me through

My black pearl

You are a very

Important resource in my life

I Am Me

My physical traits

Are not a factor

Not my full sensual lips

Nor my voluptuous breasts

Not my coke bottle shaped hips

Nor my seductive brown eyes

What matters are my talents

And how my mind works

What matter is how I treat people

And how I handle and cope with stress

What matters is that I educate my mind

And how I let my mind lead me down a great path

My short, black, silk hair

Doesn't matter

My smooth, brown skin

Is not an issue

My height and weight
Shouldn't be important

What should be important
Is that I walk with pride

What should matter
Is that I am very determined to get what I want

What should matter
Is that I am strong willed and I will let nothing stop me

My physical traits
Shouldn't be an issue

What should be important
Is that I'm determined, strong willed
And will never give up on my destiny

Meeting of Strangers

Was this by chance

The meeting of these

Two strangers

Could it have been fate

Or could it have

Been destiny

The meeting of these strangers

Happened through friends

They didn't know where this could lead

They didn't know

When this started

Or where this could end

The strangers didn't

Know they could

Fall in love instantly

Could this have

Been luck or

Was it meant to be

Did they toss pennies

Or was it a message

In a bottle just for them

The meeting didn't happen

By chance nor

Was it fate

The meeting of

These two strangers

Truly was destined

They didn't toss pennies

Nor did they

Wish upon a star

They waited patiently

On God and

God brought them together

These two strangers

Are strangers no more

And now are planning a life together

They have their

Future and their

Life ahead of them

Intimate Hearts

Two intimate hearts

That is intertwined

Sharing their souls

That is so divine

Two intimate hearts

Coming together

And any storm

They know they can weather

Two intimate hearts

That has fallen in love

Deep within

Not far from above

Two intimate hearts

The heart it sees

From all the pain and hurt

It must be set free

Two intimate hearts

That is intertwined

Sharing their souls

That is so divine

The Wedding Poem

I'm watching and waiting
As you march down the aisle

I'm watching and waiting
For you to be mine

I can imagine how nervous you were
As you slipped on your beautiful white gown

I can see you putting make up
On your already gorgeous skin

I can see you putting on your veil
With such ease and carefulness

Today is our day
Our day to be happy

Today is our day
Our day to commit to each other

Today is our day
Our day to say our 'I do's'

I do love you
And that love will last forever

I do honor you

I will honor you and never hurt you

I do commit to you

I commit my mind, body, soul, and spirit to you

Our future begins now

Our future begins with us being together

The future, our future

Begins with us, our commitment to each other

I'm marching down the aisle

To the man God gave me

I'm marching down the aisle

To the man who is totally devoted to me

I see a handsome man

Patiently waiting and watching

As I look at you

I can imagine how nervous you are

I can hear the thoughts

That is running through your head

Will we be able

To make one another happy

Or maybe you are asking yourself

Will this really work

I can simply answer

These and other questions

Things are not always going to be easy

Things are not going to always be hard

As long as we help

And love one another

Baby this I do

I commit myself to you

I commit myself

To loving your good and bad points

I commit myself

To helping you even if you don't ask

I commit myself

To caring for you when you're well and when you're sick

There will be days
When we will have our ups

There will be days
When we will have our downs

The minister is holding
Our rings and blessing us

He's blessing the journey
That we are about to embark upon together as one

He's blessing the children
That we will one day have

There is no one else
In this world for me

We will have the rest our lives
To share in each other's love

I thank God everyday
For you coming into my life

As long as we keep God first
Things will work out

Will You Love Me

Will you love

Me for me

Will you love

Me when I

Don't feel like cooking

Will you love

Me when I

Don't want to iron your clothes

Will you love

Me when I

Don't want to run your bath water

Will you love

Me when I

Don't quite keep the house clean

Will you love

Me when I

Cry for no reason

Will you love

Me when I

Smile uncontrollably

Will you love

Me when I

Am well

Will you love

Me when I

Am sick

Will you love

Me when I

Don't want sex

Will you love

Me when I

Don't want to be touched

Will you love

Me when I

Fall flat on my face

Will you love

Me when I

Rise up

Will you love

Me when I

Am angry

Will you love

Me when I

Am sad

Simply asked

Will you love

Me for me

Will you love

Me when I

Argue with you

Will you love

Me when I

Don't want to be bothered

Will you love

Me when I

Burn your food

Will you love

Me when I

Dress conservatively

Will you love

Me when I

Dress sexy

Will you love

Me when I

Am loud

Will you love

Me when I

Am too quiet

Will you love

Me when I

Scream out loud

Will you love

Me when I

Keep things hidden inside

Simply asked

Will you love

Me for me

I Let Go

I let go
Of all my inabilities
And of my insecurities

Of all my heartaches
And of all my pain

Of all my worries
And of all my troubles

I let go
Of needing your approval
And of needing your opinions

Of everything
And of everybody

Of needing a man
And of needing validation

I let go
Of compromising my thoughts
And of compromising my ways

Of being alone
And of being lonely

Of the past

And of the hurt
I now have freedom

Freedom
To be an imperfect woman
In an imperfect world

To say what I want to say
To do what I want to do

To feel love
To give love

Freedom
To reach my goals
To strive for perfection

To be myself
To love myself

To be real
Not to compromise me

I have let go
Of everything and everybody
And in turn
I have gained freedom
For myself

Independent Woman

No one in

No one out

Don't bring me gifts

Nor bring me charity

I can stand alone

On these two feet of mine

I don't want your help

Nor do I need you

My walls are up

And they're not coming down

My heart is no longer for the taking

And neither am I

Are you getting the picture

You are no longer welcomed

So let me make it clear

And painfully obvious

I am an independent woman

Who doesn't need your help

It's Not About You

My life

My terms

My way

It's not about you

Wanting to take

Care of me

Needing me to

Depend solely on you

The love that you

Think you can give me

It's not about you

The happiness that you

Think you can give me

Trying to fill

A void that isn't there

Trying to complete me

Or trying to satisfy me

It's my life

My terms

My way

I don't need you

To make me happy

Or to satisfy me

The void that you

Want to fill

Has already been filled

My happiness no longer

Depends on you

Or anyone for that matter

My independence is

My own personal freedom

From this the male's ego

The love that I have

Is the love that I

Have for myself

My life

My terms

My way

This is what you

Will have to accept

It's not about you

It's all about me baby

Since I Knew You Were Coming

Since I knew you were coming

I took time to prepare

And I did everything

With love and with care

Since I knew you were coming

I must admit I was nervous

But I took time and

Did everything with great service

Since I knew you were coming

I took the time to think

About how sometimes you might fall

But I'll never let you sink

Since I knew you were coming

I had some thoughts

In case I'm ever mad with you

I'll remember my short comings and my faults

Since I knew you were coming

I talked to friends

And they told how to

Prepare for you hours on end

Since I knew you were coming

I sat and I thought

How I had to teach you

To yourself you had to be true

Since I knew you were coming

I knew I had to tell you how special you are

And no one could replace you

No one by far

Since I knew you were coming

I took time to prepare

And I did everything

With love and with care

Sister

Sister, what an amazing word

A word that only a special person can wear

Sister, a title only held by a marvelous person

Let me tell you what a sister is

A sister is someone who is strong

When you are weak

A sister is a person

Who gives you advice

Even when you don't want it

A sister is a person

Who always have a shoulder

For you to cry on

A sister is a person

Who encourages you

In your darkest hour

A sister is a person

Who loves you

No matter what foolish things you've done

Sister all of this describes you

But wait there's more

There's a word, a word that I can't find that defines you

This word

The word that I can't find

Describes your character

This word

That I can't find

Goes beyond sisterhood

This word

Best describe your

Character as being strong

Yes sister

You are

A strong, black woman

This word

Best describes your

Character as being caring

Even when a person hurts you

You still manage somehow

To care for them

This word

Best describe your

Character as being loving

Yes sister

You are a

Loving, giving person

One day I may

Find the word

That best describes you

But for now

This is what

I want you to know

Sister there is

A special bond

That the two of us share

This special bond

Is a bond

That cannot be broken

What we share

Goes above and beyond

Our bond of sisterhood

Sister we have

Something that no one else

In this world have

Sister I have you

And you have me

And nobody can break that special bond

Thank you for being

The sister I needed

I love you

Your Love Is

Your love is

Like the dew

That wets me

And lets me know

I'm still here

Your love is

Like is a broom

That sweeps away

All of my

Troubles and fears

Your love is

Like a friend

That lifts me

When I'm down

And cheers me

When I'm sad

Your love is

Like a book

That opens up

And teaches me the

Things I need to know

Your love is

Like a butterfly

One that has a

Vivid personality

Your love is

Like a pair

Of eyes that

Is beautiful and

Full of amazement

Your love is

Like the sunshine

That brightens

My soul and

Delights my heart

Your love is

Like a pair of

Hands I can hold

When I'm all alone

Your love is

Like a rock

That stays and

Never moves

Your love is

Like a kiss

That softly touches

My brown skin

And say

I love you

Your love is

Like a gentle hug

That let's me

Know that you

Care for me

Missing You

Sitting here missing you

Sitting here thinking of you

The days we talked on the phone

The days we walked side by side

The way you've enlightened me

The way you've delighted me

The times that you have been there

The times that you showed that you care

Doesn't that give you a clue

That I'm sitting here missing you

To True Blue

Here's to true blue

I believe that's you

I looked and looked

And could find no other

Truer than you

Here's to a friend that's true blue

I searched and searched

For someone who know

That being friends means being true blue

I couldn't find that someone until I met you

Here's to a friend that's true blue

Someone who I know will stay until the end

Here's to true blue

I know now that it's you

Always stay true blue

And never change

Always stay true blue

And you will always have someone to love you

No One Special

I'm no one special

As you can see

I don't have a cry

And I don't have a plea

I'm no one special

This really isn't hard to explain

But I guess

I can't complain

I'm no one special

Even though I have to sigh

But that's alright

I don't worry neither do I cry

I'm no one special

Don't try to cheer me up

I will just sit here

And just sulk

I'm no one special

I've made that plainly clear

So throw a party

And plan a cheer

I'm no one special

I laugh, work, and play

To you I'm just someone

Who doesn't have words to say

I'm no one special

I sit around

And watch t.v.

Everyone knows that I very lonely

I'm no one special

Making friends here

Losing friends there

Trying to find someone to be sincere

I'm no one special

Without a gift

Without a talent

Just someone the wind tends to shift

I'm no one special

No one cares

Some don't love me

Some don't share

I'm no one special

No one spending time

To talk to me

Saying you're all mine

I'm no one special

As you can see

I don't have a cry

And I don't have a plea

Shy Day

I was sitting alone in the park one day

And that's when I saw him from across the way

He had big brown eyes that captured my heart

I had fallen in love with him right from the start

I wonder if he knew how special he was

To me he wasn't just another cause

I was sitting there hoping he would notice me

But another pretty girl was all he could see

When I had finally given up hope

That's when he came and sat down and spoke

"Hey how are you doing?" he began to say

While he was speaking I began wishing he'd go away

He introduced himself as Juan

But I could care less if it was Juan or Don

He began to ask what was my name

I looked and acted as if I was shame

He looked and then he smiled

I was still wishing he'd go away all the while

I asked him who was the girl he was talking to

He said he was ending a relationship that was long overdue

I gave a shy kind of smile

Maybe this one will go the extra mile

He began to start a conversation

But in talking department I showed no cooperation

I looked into his beautiful brown eyes

They were as clear as the skies

The expression on his face

Showed such style and grace

He only stood about five feet tall

But his physique was not at all small

I begin to wonder what he will say next

What type of questions will he ask

His face was big and bold

But a whole different story it had told

It seemed the ending of the relationship was the other way around

He looked as if his heart had fell to the ground

I had asked what was wrong

But all he could do was sing a sad song

I touched him on the shoulder and told him not to cry

But all he did was look at me and deeply sighed

I tried everything that I thought would help

But he had much too much pity on himself

I grabbed by the hand

And we both began to stand

I told him to come and let's take a walk

And that's when we began to seriously talk

I began to ask "What's wrong with you?"

He answered "Nothing I can't get through."

I squeezed his hand and told him not to worry

That's when he begin to tell his story

I listened trying not to shed a tear

But the things he said put in me a little fear

I looked into his eyes and they were full of hurt

 The things I said to him didn't seem to work

He was full of rage and hate

But his story I could not escape

His childhood story he had told

Rage is what he continued to show

He said he stood and watched his mother get shot

That sort of thing no one will ever be able to block

He was telling his story to a complete stranger

Somehow I knew I wasn't in any danger

He began telling me that never learned my name

I apologized and explained that wasn't playing any games

He continued his story

And I continued to see his fury

He kept saying maybe there was something he could have done

I tried my best to keep him calm

He was getting angrier by the second

Even his looks became very hesitant

While telling his story I began to have some doubt

But then I thought what if that was me and I cast it out

We could tell the day was ending

As so was the talk that was very friendly

I laid my head to rest

On his big broad chest

My long black hair he began to caress

His gentle touch was at its best

As we sat on the beach and watched the golden sun

We both wondered where each other came from

I don't know where this could lead

But as we go along we shall see

To My Friend

As I sit and look out the window

I think of how you have helped me

When all others failed

You were there to tell

Me how to make it

As I sit and look out the window

I don't know how or when

Our friendship began

You were there through thick and thin

You stood by me even until the end

As I sit and look out the window

I think of how you

Sat there and listened to all of my problems

You even heard the good things

When I needed someone to lean on you were right there

There are so many things you did for me

There are so many things you said to me

There were so many times you were there for me

And the only thing I can say is this

Thank you for everything you said and done for me.

To My True Love

To my true love

To you and you only do I give my love

To you and you only do I give my heart

You have lighted my way

You have always stayed in my heart

You have always stayed in my soul

Your beautiful eyes

Your calm smile

Your peaceful way of talking

Your graceful way of walking

To my true love

To you and you only

Do I give my love

The Van Lady

The van lady

That's what most folks say

The van lady

She lives right each and everyday

The van lady

Loves like the Bible say you should

The van lady

People try to spot her life

The van lady

Everybody knows she lives right

The van lady

She's lowly and meek at heart

The van lady

She's been like that from start

The van lady

Everybody knows and everybody sees

The van lady

Is holy and clean

How Could I

How could I not see

How wrong you were for me

People tried their best to tell me

But I didn't want to see

Just how wrong I could be

I stood for you

I fought for you

And you still proved me wrong

You did nothing for me

You did not fight for me

Now I'm going to find a man

That really loves me

One that will be there

In the late midnight hour

One that will

Dry my every tear

I loved you

But you hated me

I gave you my heart

And you gave me heartache

I gave you support

And you knocked me down

I committed the sin

Of committing to you

I trusted lust

Instead of trusting love

I gave you all of me

And you gave me nothing of you

Instead of saying don't worry

You caused me grief

You are nothing

But trouble, heartache, and pain

I've Been

I've been criticized

I've been denied

But I took it all in stride

I've been hurt

I've been blamed

But I'm not ashamed

I've been put down

I've been let down

But I will not fall to the ground

I've been convicted

I've been restricted

But I'll always remain committed

Happiness is a stranger

I feel as though

My life is in danger

Peace no longer dwells

And so many are

Waiting for me to fail

My life is getting to be so insane

But my words

I will not restrain

Everything is moving so fast

But I'm looking towards the future

Rather than past

This world is so hard to escape

But I dare not leave

My life up to fate

Connection

There's a connection
Between the two of us

It's not about our brown skin
Merging together as one

It's not about our eyes
Meeting across any crowded room

This connection has
Put us another plane

With this connection
Our minds can unite together

With this connection
Our souls can intertwine

There's a connection
Between the two of us

This connection is something
That leaves you speechless

It's not about the two of us
Hugging one another

It's not about the two of us

Kissing one another

This connection between us

Is something that we can share together

This connection is about the two of us

Being intimately connected

There's nothing about

Our connection that is weak

There's nothing about

Our connection that can be torn down

This connection has strengthen us

Well beyond the breaking point

This connection that is between us

Allows us to reach each other without leaving home

This connection that is between us

Allows me to close my eyes and see your face

There is this connection

Between the two of us

One that allows our souls and

Our minds to intertwine

Strong Love

I want to run to you

I want to tell you so bad that I love you

I want to say to you

I love you

I love you with a powerful love

I love you with a strong love

I want to say to you

I love you with an unstoppable love

The type of love that move mountains

The type of love that has a hold on me and won't let me go

I want to say to you

You are the first person I think about when I wake up

You are the last person on my mind before bed

I want to say to you

You make me smile when I want to cry

I want to say to you

With each passing second

I fall deeper and deeper in love with you

I have never

Loved someone so much before

It is something that stirs my soul

It is something that pricks my very being

Never Ending

I have a
Never ending passion

This passion is something
I cannot just make go away

Your smile and
Your laugh has created this passion

When I look around
I see no one but you

When I think
I think of no one but you

I have this
Never ending passion for you

Sometimes I don't know
Exactly what to do

This passion is something
That burns day and night
You mean the world to me
And I wish I could express this to you

I have never had

This type of passion

The type of passion

That won't let you love anyone else

No matter whom I am with

You will always be the one I missed out on

Because of this passion

I want to be something you could never be

When I get quiet with you

It's because I'm thinking of you

This passion won't let me

Love anyone else but you

Because of this passion

I want to scream your name from the mountain top

Oh how I wish you

Knew just how much passion I have for you

I have this

Never ending passion

This type of passion

I don't want to leave my heart

Because with this passion

I will always carry you with me

This never ending passion

Is something I don't want to ever end

My Heart

My heart is aching

My head is pounding

My soul is as transparent as glass

Yet you cannot you see through it to see

My feelings for you

My feet want to run to you

My arms want to hold you

My eyes want to behold you

My ears want to listen to you

My mind is constantly thinking of you

My mouth is ready to utter the words 'I love you'

I tell you everyday how I feel

And yet you do not recognize

How do I tell you that you are

The one I want

How do I fix my mouth to say 'I love you'

Why do I have feelings for you

Why do I love you so much

There is something special about you

There is something that lies

Within you that I need and want

My soul is as transparent as glass

And yet you cannot see far enough

Through it to see that I love you

My Love For You

I tried to forget about you

But the love I have for you is too strong

My words are not

Enough to express to you

This love is so strong

That it has given me

What I have never had

It's given me something I have longed for

It has given me freedom

The freedom to be just who I am

It has given me the courage

The courage to truly fall in love

It has given me strength

The strength to be your friend when I can't be your lover

It has given me hope

The hope that someday you will fall in love with me

The love I have for you

Surpasses any love I have ever had for anyone

It conquers any and every fear

It penetrates me in a way no one ever has before

Do I dare give up this love

Do I dare let you go

Should I continue to love you

Should I move on and not look back

You have done a wonderful thing for me

You have set me free

You have given me courage and

You have given me strength

I have come to the realization

Of a lot of things

But there is one important fact

I have realized

A lover you cannot be

A husband you dare not be

But a true friend and

A brother you are

I Know

I know that you can't be my lover

I know that you can't be my husband

The only thing you can be is my friend

I know we are only meant to be friends

I know you take my breath away

I know you sweep me off my feet

I know you make my heart jump into my throat each time I see you

I know when I think about you I smile from ear to ear

I know when you speak to me my heart fills with joy

I know when I hear you sing a song I fall deeper and deeper in love with you

I know when I see you in a suit I melt

I know my heart and soul belongs to you

I know I want to share my life with you

I know I want to share my dreams with you

I know I want to share my ups and downs with you

I know when I hear you laugh I feel special

I know that I love you very much

I know that when I am around you troubles disappear

I know you make my spirit soar

I know you set my soul on fire

I know that my love for you will never change

Instantly

I thought that maybe

I was moving too fast

I thought you were

A figment of my imagination

When I heard your voice

When I saw your smile

I knew instantly

There was no letting go

I love you very much

And trust me

I won't let go of you

You are what I want

I will never break your heart

Nor will I ever hurt you

The only thing

I want to do is love you

Instantly I knew

You were for me

Instantly I knew

I wanted you

I Thought About You

I thought about you today

That should be nothing unusual

I thought about the way you sound

When you talk or sing to me

I thought about the way

I fell in love with you

I ask myself

Everyday how did this happen

I do not regret

Being in love with you

I just have to know

How did this happen

I thought about you today

I thought about how you fill my heart

When I thought about you

I thought about how you make me

Feel good even to the core of my soul

Am I supposed to

Be in love with you

I thought about you today

How you have been an amazing asset in my life

I thought about you today

I thought about your words of wisdom

You are always willing to share

Am I supposed to abandon

These feelings that has pierced my soul

Am I supposed to give up

On the love that I have for you

I thought about you today

I thought about the way you make me feel

I thought about you today

I thought about everything that makes you who you are

I Broke My Mine Own Heart

Today I broke my own heart

I realized that holding on to

Someone and something I want

Is not good for me

Today I broke mine own heart

I made the mistake of telling you that I love you

I couldn't hold that big secret to myself

I couldn't hide the expressions from you any longer

Today I broke mine own heart

I expected you to say 'Baby I love you too'

Every time I speak with you I want to utter those words

I told you everything and hid nothing

Today I broke mine own heart

By confessing to things I didn't want you to know

By being so honest with you that it even scared me

By hiding or omitting nothing from you

Today I broke mine own heart

I told everyone that I had fallen in love with you

I thought that by doing so

You would enter a relationship with me

Today I broke mine own heart

I realized today that I have to let you go

I realized that holding on to you is not doing me any good

I realized that there is only one way you see me and that is as a friend

Today I broke mine own heart

I made the mistake of telling you that

I was truly in love with you

I made the mistake of wanting you

Today I broke mine own heart

You Are the Man

You are the man of my dreams

You are the man in my dreams

You are the one that I want to hear 'I love you' from

You are the one that I want to hold me

You are the one whose chest I want to place my head

You are the one whose neck I want to hug

You are the one whose arms I want wrapped around me

You are the one whose hands I want to touch me

You are the one I want to hear sing a song

You are the one whose laughter I want to hear

You are the one whose smile I love to see

You are the one whose life I want to share

You are the one that makes my heart be still

You are the one that makes me take a deep breath

You are the one that makes my spirit soar

You are the one that set me free

You are the one I have to let go of

You are the one I have to love from a distance

You are the one I must move on from

You are the one I want and cannot have

Ecstasy

Sweet taste of your lips

Gentle touch of your hands

Passionate kisses

Our brown skin connecting with one another

Strong arms wrapped around me

Sweet nothings whispered in my ear

I'm longing for you

I'm longing to touch and taste you

Your love transcends me

Your love sends me to pure ecstasy

I'm Ready

I'm ready

To love you

To give my body and soul to you

I'm ready

To spend the rest of my life with you

To stop running from you

I'm ready

To let go of everyone else

To give in to you

I'm ready

For everything you have to offer me

For the peace of mind you offer

I'm ready

For the opportunities and benefits being in love with you has to offer

For the trials and tribulation of being in love with you that comes along with it

I'm ready

For you

And only you baby

Requited Love

The love I have for you
Gets under my skin
I love you so much
It feels as though it's a sin

How can I keep it
Away from you
How can I think of it
And not be true

My love is here
And it's not going away
My love is true
And I need you to stay

You are the best
Thing to ever happened to me
Your love has
Truly set me free

Preach on preacher
Sing on choir
This love is enough
To set my soul on fire

I love you too much

To ever leave you alone

I love you too much

To be anything less than strong

Essence of love

Heart pounding

Head spinning

I'm in love with you

Feet running

Arms aching

I want to hold you

Mind wondering

Eyes searching

Just don't let me go

Soul soaring

Spirit flying

Uplifted to the highest heights

I need you

I love you

I want you

Heart pounding

Head spinning

I'm in love with you

Can't Let You Go

I feel your presence

I feel your arms around me

I can hear your laughter

I can see your smile

I can hear the sweet sound of your voice

I can even hear you sing my favorite song

I can't let you go

Or maybe it's that I won't let you go

I tried to forget about you

I tried to cast you out of my mind

You have invaded my heart

You have invaded my soul

It feels as though you a piece of my heart

You have a piece of my soul

I am not willing to let you go

I am not willing to let you get away

Thinking About You

I think about you

When I wake up

I think about you

When I go to bed

I think about you

When I'm all alone

I think about you

When I'm in a crowded room

I think about you

Every day and every night

I think about you

When I try to think of someone else

I think about you

When I can't be near you

I think about you

When I'm next to you

I think about you

When I want to cry

I think about you

When I want to smile

Secret Love

Why is it I feel
This way for you

Having these feelings
And being able to tell you
Is hurting me

I want you but
I know I can't have you

I want to tell you
But I dare not speak of it

Why do I love you
This way

Why do I
Dare not let go of you

I can't destroy
The friendship that we have

You make me smile
When I want to cry

You make me laugh

When no one can

You pray for me

When I can't pray for myself

I always think

About you when I don't think about myself

You consume my thoughts

You have consumed my heart

No matter who I am with

You will be the one I'll always love

You'll always be my secret lover

And you and the love I have for you I will keep to myself

I can't pursue you

And I definitely can't have you

What am I suppose

To do about the love I have

Am I to hold to it

Am I to let it go

I want to tell you

Exactly how I feel

But you are what I want

And someone I can't have

Here I Stand

Here I stand

In the arms of a man

One that will love me

And hold my hand

Here I stand

In the arms of a man

One that will accept me

For who I am

Here I stand

In the arms of a man

One that will encourage me

To do the best I can

Here I stand

In the arms of a man

One that will hold me

And never let me go

Here I stand

In the arms of the man

One that is strong

And won't let me fall

Here I stand

In the arms of a man

One who cares for me

And gives me solace

Here I stand

In the arms of a man

One that will love me

And hold my hand

Letting Go

Letting go of you

Is easier said than done

I don't want to

Give up this love

Letting go of you

Has not even entered my mind

This is something that

Is hard for me to define

I know you said that

There was someone better

I know you said to

Let you go

I think about day and night

Tell me how am I supposed to

Let go of the very thing

The very person that makes me happy

I can't let you go

I can't turn off these feelings for you

In my dreams I see you

Now I am in love with you and

I don't want to let go of this love

Your eyes are full of passion

Your mouth speak sweet words

Your walk is nonchalant

Your talk is smooth

Letting go of you

Will never be easy

Letting go of you

Is something I don't really want to do

How Can I

How can we be so close

And yet we are so far

We share the same interests

We share the same common goals

We share our laughs together

You even pray for me when I need it

I want to share my life with you

I want to grow old with you

We share so many thoughts with each other

We even share our own private jokes

How can we sing to each other

And not sing our true love song

How can I be in love with you

And you not be in love with me

I want to emulate my love

I want to hold on to you tightly

This love has overtaken my heart

This love has engulfed my soul

You have become a part of me

You have completely taken over my life

Don't Let Go

Touch me

Hold me

Don't let go

Need me

Long for me

Don't let go

Love me

Kiss me

Don't let go

Laugh with me

Cry with me

Don't let go

Touch me

Hold me

Don't let go

I Cannot

I cannot count the ways

That I love you

Because my love for you is too great

I cannot wish upon a star

Because to have you in my life

Is a wish that is too great to make

I want to

Satisfy the part of you

That no one else has ever touched

I can no longer

Hide the way I feel for you

I want our love to connect on another level

You are more than

A true man to me

So many times over

I cannot count the ways

That I love you

Because my love for you is too great